TIME DON'T WAIT FOR NOBODY

by

THEODIA HENRY

DEDICATION

To the corners that raised me,

The blocks that taught me pain before I even knew fear, and the nights that whispered survival in my ear.

To my fallen soldiers — Dameon, Jimmy Shoe Barker, Jermaine "Pooh" Barker, and all the ones whose names are etched in my heart. You left too soon, but your spirit rides with me every day. I carry you in every move, every choice, every breath.

To my mama, Bridget, who held me when the world tried to break me,

And to Granny Flora, whose hands and heart built me before the streets could try to tear me down.

To anyone who's been counted out, left behind, or told they wouldn't make it —

This book is for you. The grind don't stop, the streets don't sleep, and neither should your fire.

To my family, my blood, my legacy — I see you, I honor you, I rise because of you.

— Theodia Martell Henry

CONTENTS

CHAPTER ONE:

Blood, Sweat, Silence

The streets don't give second chances — Theodis learned that early, long before he understood what survival really demanded. Nights blurred into mornings, the corners stayed alive with whispered deals and quiet threats, and the only currency that mattered was respect. Time was both endless and fleeting, a cruel paradox that tested anyone bold enough to step into its rhythm. Every siren, every shout, every flicker of neon felt like a reminder that nothing waited for anyone.

He wasn't born into riches or comfort. His life had always been movement — chaos, noise, and the constant grind of people hustling just to keep a roof over their heads. From a young age, Theodis knew the world wouldn't hand him anything for free. His mama, Bridget, worked double shifts, sacrificing sleep and comfort to keep him grounded, always repeating the same words, like a mantra: "Son, time don't wait for nobody. You better make yours count." At first, Theodis nodded as he understood, but those words were just sounds in the air, whispers that would only sink in much later, after enough nights of watching dreams slip away for lack of action.

Theodis was smart — street smart before anything else. He could read people like worn pages of a diary: the ones who were loyal, the ones who were dangerous, and the ones who would crumble under pressure. He could smell lies in a voice, detect weakness in a glance. But street smarts only went so far. Life had a way of flipping everything upside down in an instant. One wrong move, one delayed decision, one second too slow, and everything could change — sometimes forever. He had seen it too many times, watched boys younger than him vanish into a world of pain, arrested, hurt, or worse.

He wasn't looking for trouble, yet trouble had an uncanny way of finding him. Every corner seemed to whisper lessons, each harder than the last. Some lessons were paid in sweat, some in blood, some in silence — the kind that settles deep in your chest when you realize exactly how much you've lost. Loss wasn't just about possessions. It was about friendships severed, opportunities gone, trust broken, and pieces of yourself you didn't even know you'd given away until they were gone.

Despite the chaos, despite the noise and the constant push to survive, there was always a voice in his head — his mama's voice — reminding him that time never stopped for anyone. And the older he got, the louder it echoed, as if the city itself amplified her words. It was a voice that both haunted and guided him, pushing him forward, daring him to outrun the streets before they consumed him entirely.

Theodis had learned quickly: the streets demanded respect, intelligence, and courage — a kind of courage that didn't always feel natural. And beneath the grit, beneath the blaring horns and shouting corners, he realized life wasn't just about surviving. It was about making every second count, even when the world seemed determined to erase you.

And somewhere in the shadows, he felt a spark — a tiny flame of ambition, a whisper that maybe he could rise above the chaos, maybe he could bend time itself in his favor, if only he had the strength and the wit to seize it. But the city had its own rules, and it would not wait for dreams. Only the vigilant, the cunning, and the fearless could hope to survive.

Theodis took a deep breath, letting the night air fill his lungs, and stepped forward. Another corner, another choice, another gamble. Blood, sweat, and silence. The streets demanded their due, but Theodis was ready to pay — and ready to take what the world had denied him if he could survive long enough to claim it.

CHAPTER TWO:

Stakes in the Shadows

Morning light hit differently when you hadn't slept. Theodis leaned against the cracked brick wall outside the corner store, feeling the rough surface dig into his back as the city stretched awake around him. Cars rolled slow, their engines growling through the morning fog. Music hummed low from passing rides, and the scent of syrup from street vendors mingled with the sharp tang of smoke from last night's fires. Everything seemed alive, watching, judging, waiting.

He hadn't been out partying or chasing thrills — no, he had been thinking. About how life moved faster than anyone could catch it. About how some people got chances handed to them, and some had to carve their own from nothing but grit, determination, and hope. Theodis had always belonged to the latter category.

The hustle started small. A favor here, a delivery there. Nothing flashy, nothing illegal, he couldn't handle. Word spread quickly — Theodis handled business. No drama, no mess. Just a man doing what he had to do to survive. In the streets, reputation was currency, and Theodis was stacking his with quiet precision. Every nod, every whispered acknowledgment, every small trust he earned was another brick in the foundation he was building.

But hustling wasn't just about money — it was about understanding the game. Watching how power moved, how respect shifted from person to person, and how loyalty could be bought, traded, or broken in an instant. He studied the older guys with their flashy cars, gold chains catching the weak morning light, and loud, confident talk. Most of them were just playing a role, pretending to be more than they were. Theodis took notes silently, memorizing every lesson the streets offered. He didn't want to look rich; he wanted to be smart.

Temptation, however, was always close. Easy money whispered from every dark alley, every quiet corner. Danger walked hand-in-hand with opportunity, a shadow that followed every move he made. The first time he saw a friend caught up in the wrong game, it hit him like a punch to the chest. Not just the loss, but the stark realization that every choice, every move, had a countdown clock. One slip, one hesitation, one wrong glance, and everything could collapse.

He started thinking about "getting out." Could someone really leave the streets that raised them? Could you step away from the life that molded your every instinct, your every decision, without losing yourself entirely? Theodis didn't know the answer yet, but he knew he had to find one — before time made the choice for him.

One night, counting a small stack of bills under a flickering light, Theodis paused. The money looked good, the weight of it solid in his hand. But something inside him felt empty, hollow, as though each note was a piece of his soul he was trading for temporary wins. The streets had given him skill, reputation, and survival, but at what cost?

For the first time, he whispered it aloud, a mantra that had echoed in his mama's voice for years, now claiming space in his own mind:

"Time don't wait for nobody, man. Not even me."

That moment marked a shift. The hustle was still alive, relentless and unforgiving, but something deeper stirred within Theodis — a hunger not just for survival, but for meaning. Something that demanded more than quick wins, more than respect earned on street corners and whispered transactions. A fire was lighting inside him, one that the streets themselves might not be ready to handle.

And as the city stretched awake, Theodis straightened his shoulders and stepped off the curb. Another day, another choice, another risk. Stakes in the shadows, but he was ready — ready to play the game, ready to see just how far he could go without losing himself completely.

CHAPTER THREE:

Lessons Paid in Full

Time has a way of teaching lessons money can't buy. And for Theodis, those lessons came hard — one after another, like relentless waves crashing against a fragile shore, never pausing, never forgiving.

He started losing people. Not just friends — brothers. The ones who laughed with him, rode with him, shared meals when food was scarce. One by one, they disappeared — some swallowed by the system, some consumed by the streets, and some taken permanently, buried in the dirt.

Each loss left a hollow in his chest, a void that no hustle, no stack of bills, could fill.

The first loss hit like a hammer, leaving him breathless with shock. The second broke something deeper inside, a fracture that no time could mend. By the third, Theodis stopped pretending that pain got easier with practice. It didn't. Grief didn't come in waves; it was a storm that refused to leave, settling in his bones and shaping him whether he liked it or not.

Nights became quieter. The corners he used to stand on, the streets that once pulsed with life, began to feel haunted — echoes of laughter replaced by whispers of absence. Every sound reminded him that time wasn't just moving forward; it was taking. The slam of a car door, the wail of a siren, the silent buzz of a phone that never rang — all reminders that the world moved on without pause, without care.

Theodis tried to keep busy, throwing himself into the hustle, counting bills, making moves. But no amount of money, motion, or reputation could silence the truth: life was short, fragile, and unpredictable. One evening, he found himself staring at old photographs, the faces of those who once smiled big, who once believed tomorrow would come. Some of them never saw twenty-

five. Some never made it to twenty-one. Their eyes, frozen in film, seemed to stare back at him, accusing, reminding, haunting.

One night, sitting alone on his porch with a half-empty bottle and a full heart of regret, Theodis whispered to the dark, "They're gone, and time just keeps running like it don't care." And in that moment, the truth hit him like a bullet — time didn't care. It never slowed down for heartbreak, never paused for grief, never lingered for anyone. It just moved, steady, cold, and true.

That realization changed him. He began to pull back from old habits, not out of fear, but out of awareness. He started guiding younger dudes on the block, pulling them aside to share truths he wished someone had told him when he was their age.

"Don't waste years proving something to people who won't remember your name in ten," he'd say. Some listened. Most didn't. But even planting one seed felt like a victory. Every word, every lesson, was a small rebellion against the streets' relentless tide, a chance to give someone a head start he never had.

Every loss had a lesson. Every scar told a story. Pain became more than an enemy; it became a teacher. And as the heaviness settled, a new purpose began to rise — slow, steady, undeniable. For the first time, Theodis thought about something he never thought possible:

peace. Not the fleeting calm of a quick payday, but a deeper, quieter sense of survival, understanding, and finally, control.

The path ahead was still long, winding, and dangerous. But for the first time, Theodis felt ready to walk it with intention, knowing that time wouldn't wait — and neither would he.

CHAPTER FOUR:

Crossroads of Change

Change didn't come easy when the streets had your name carved in concrete. Theodis had lived fast, seen too much, and lost enough to know that standing still was just another way to fall behind. Every corner, every alley, every echo of the city reminded him of the life he once lived — the choices made, the risks taken, the people lost.

One morning, before the sun even dared to touch the skyline, Theodis woke to a city still wrapped in quiet. For once, he didn't reach for his phone, his chain, or the plans he had mapped for the day. He just sat there, shoulders heavy but still, listening. The silence was thick, almost tangible, but it felt... peaceful. And in that rare stillness, he realized something profound: peace wasn't about the noise stopping — it was about finding your calm in the middle of it.

The old him had chased money, respect, and fleeting moments of thrill. The new him wanted something different. He wanted meaning. But stepping away from the streets wasn't simple. When you change, people notice. Old friends question your loyalty. Some whisper that you've gone soft. Others assume you're acting brand new, playing a part. But Theodis didn't feel the need to prove anything anymore. He wasn't trying to impress anyone. He was trying to live.

He started small — helping out at a local youth center. Nothing flashy, nothing designed to make headlines. Just talking to the kids, telling stories, sharing the truths the streets had taught him. At first, they laughed. They saw the tattoos, the scars, the history etched into his skin, and assumed he was just another man preaching after a life of mistakes. But as he spoke, their laughter faded. They listened because he spoke their language — not from books or lessons, but from experience forged in blood, sweat, and survival.

He told them about time — how it moved, whether you moved with it or not. How chasing the fast life was really just running in circles, exhausting yourself for temporary highs. How regret didn't strike all at once — it crept in slowly, year by year, until one day you realize you spent half your life surviving but never truly living.

Some nights, Theodis still wrestled with his past — the faces, the memories, the mistakes he could never undo. But each time, he reminded himself that every scar was proof he had survived. Proof that even in the darkest corners, he had endured.

One evening, one of the kids asked him, eyes wide and earnest, "OG, you ever wish you could go back?"

Theodis smiled, a quiet sadness in the curve of his lips, and said, "Sometimes... but then I remember — time don't wait for anybody. If I went back, I'd miss where I'm going."

That moment stuck with him, lingering long after the lights dimmed and the kids went home. He was still healing. He was still learning. But for the first time, Theodis wasn't just surviving the days — he was living them with intention, purpose, and a kind of quiet strength the streets could never take away.

And as the city stretched awake each morning, Theodis walked its streets differently now. No longer just a participant in the game, but a man aware of every choice, every second, every path. A man ready to shape his life, instead of letting the world shape him.

CHAPTER FIVE:

The House That Made Me

Before the streets, before the lessons and the losses, there was a small house that held everything together — love, noise, struggle, and family. That house was where Theodis first learned the meaning of respect, responsibility, and survival long before the world tried to teach it another way.

He grew up at his granny's place, a home that always seemed full — five aunts, two uncles, cousins everywhere, and laughter mixed with arguments, music, and prayers. The air was alive with movement. You could walk from one room to the next and hear five different stories being told at the same time, each carrying its own wisdom, its own warning, its own laughter.

His aunts — Crystal, Barbara Nell, Mary Joe, Beverly, and his mama, Bridget — ran the house like queens of a small kingdom. Each had her own voice, her own presence, and a way of teaching lessons without needing to raise it. His uncles, Sporty and Boney, were the counterbalance — tough when they needed to be, protective always, and full of that old-school grit that came from being forged by hard times and the watchful eye of their father.

And then there was his grandfather, Theodis Sr.

A man of few words but immense presence. He worked hard every day, the kind of man who didn't entertain excuses. When he came home, dinner was always ready — a sacred moment. The family gathered, heads bowed before the food, knowing that the time spent together was as important as the meal itself. Even in peace, he carried responsibility: his gun rested beside him, a silent reminder that protection was part of being a man, even in a home filled with love.

That image stayed with Theodis for life — not because it was intimidating, but because it was powerful. It showed him that being a man meant being ready, being responsible, and being aware of the world's weight without letting it crush you.

Then there was Granny Flora — the backbone of it all. She was a nurse, strong and steady, always moving, always caring. No matter how long her shift, she made sure every child was fed, every bed was made, and every soul under her roof felt safe. Her voice carried authority and calm — the kind that could stop chaos in its tracks with just one word. She was a reminder that strength wasn't always loud; sometimes it was quiet, patient, and enduring.

The house might've been crowded, but it was alive. Every night, Theodis remembered the smells of home-cooked meals — cornbread, fried chicken, spices in the air. The echoes of laughter ran through the halls long after the lights went out. The rhythm of life inside that house was chaotic but balanced, loud but tender.

It was there that Theodis learned the rhythm of family — the push and pull between struggle and love. There were lessons in every moment: how to share, how to speak up, how to listen, and most importantly, how to stand tall even when life felt unbearable.

Those days shaped him. Watching his grandfather return home, tired but steady, and watching his grandmother care for everyone before herself, planted something deep inside him. It was a belief that family was everything, that real strength came from endurance, and that no matter how hard life struck, you don't quit.

Even years later, when the streets tried to harden him, that house stayed in his heart. The smell of cornbread and fried chicken. The laughter echoes from the kitchen. The image of his grandfather at the table, unwavering and steadfast.

That house didn't just raise Theodis — it built him, brick by brick, lesson by lesson, heart by heart. It was the foundation he carried with him through every corner, every street, every gamble, and every choice the world demanded he make.

CHAPTER SIX:

Into the Streets

Every kid has that moment when the world outside the front door starts calling. For Theodis, that call came early — a whisper at first, then a rhythm, and finally a pulse that became a way of life.

That little house with Granny Flora and the whole family had kept him safe for years. Within those walls, everything had a purpose — the food, the laughter, the arguments, the lessons. But outside... the world was louder. Faster. Unforgiving. It didn't wait for anyone. It demanded respect, action, and a kind of cunning that only experience could teach.

He remembered the first time he walked past the edge of his block. The sun hung low, painting the sky in reds and golds. The older guys leaned against cars, chains glinting in the fading light, voices sharp with confidence. They moved as if the world belonged to them. To a young Theodis, that looked like freedom — like power he wanted to understand, touch, maybe even claim one day.

The first lesson his grandfather ever taught him echoed in his mind: "Pay attention, boy — the world don't play fair." He didn't understand it then. But soon enough, the streets would make him understand.

The streets had a way of testing everything Granny had taught him — patience, respect, pride. Out there, people didn't care who your family was or where you came from; they cared about what you could prove. Every day was a test of strength, courage, and wit.

Still, the lessons from home followed him like a shadow. He heard his grandmother's voice whenever he teetered on the edge of a bad decision: "Remember who you are, Theodis. Don't let the world change your heart." Those words anchored him when the streets tried to sweep him away.

At first, he stayed close to the corners, observing, listening. He wasn't there to cause trouble — he wanted to understand the rhythm, the pulse that made the streets alive. He noticed how respect moved, how power shifted, and who carried loyalty like armor. The older guys respected him not for his age, but for his quiet watchfulness. They called him "Lil Thee," after his grandfather — a name that carried a subtle power, whispered respect among those who understood.

He began running small errands, figuring out the players, learning the unspoken rules of movement. Every night, returning to that warm, crowded house, reminded him that he had something most of the kids on the block didn't — a foundation. A family that believed in him, lessons that rooted him, and a history that gave him strength.

Even when curiosity turned into risk, when he tested limits, he thought of his grandfather at the dinner table, gun resting beside him, his grandmother's hands smelling of hospital gloves and cornbread, and the sound of his mama Bridget calling, "Boy, don't forget where you came from!" He couldn't forget, not fully. That house stayed inside him — the laughter, the love, the lessons, and the discipline.

The streets were teaching him new rules now, faster, harder, colder. But Theodis was learning to play them his way — with wisdom, strategy, and patience, not just survival. And while time kept moving relentlessly forward, he began to see that every choice now would either honor where he came from... or erase it entirely.

He chose to honor it. But he never chose to accept it. The streets could shape him, test him, tempt him — but they would never define him. That was a lesson the house had built into him long before the city could try.

CHAPTER SEVEN:

The First Fall

Every story has that chapter where innocence collides with the world — where curiosity becomes choice, and the first real test arrives. For Theodis, that moment came on a morning that felt ordinary, stepping off the porch of his granny's house and into a street alive with noise, laughter, and the sharp, clattering rhythm of dice hitting the pavement.

The Moe Town Rangers held the block like kings. Their cars sat polished and gleaming under the sun, chrome rims catching every reflection like mirrors daring you to step closer. Smoke curled through the air, mingling with the low hum of music, confidence, and power. They wore their pride like armor — loud, bold, untouchable. To a young boy, it was mesmerizing.

Theodis was small but sharp. His eyes caught everything — the way hands flipped money, the way dice spun across cracked concrete, the tension and excitement in every movement. He'd stand close enough to watch, close enough to hear, but far enough not to draw attention. Something about that world pulled at him — the energy, the freedom, the danger. It was magnetic and terrifying all at once.

Every morning, he walked to Sherman Elementary with his boys, Dameon and Dante. They laughed, joked, and traded stories, trying to pretend the weight of the streets didn't follow them to school. That walk was their ritual, their tiny slice of peace before the day began, a shield against a world that demanded so much too soon.

Then there was Poopye. She had a presence that made everything else fade. Soft smile, bright eyes, books hugged tight to her chest like she carried dreams too big for the block. Every boy noticed her, but Poopye had standards. She liked clean-cut, disciplined types — basketball players, students who stayed out of trouble, sneakers fresh without a crease.

Theodis wasn't that. Not yet. He was molded by noise, chaos, and corner life — a world that fascinated and scared outsiders all at once. But when he saw Poopye, he felt a pull, a desire to be more than who he was, to rise above the label the streets had stamped on him.

In the hallway, he'd pass her, pretending not to notice, but every laugh she shared, every glance she threw, struck him differently. He wanted her attention. He wanted her respect. But more than that, he wanted to prove he was somebody — worthy of acknowledgment in a world that often ignored people like him.

Every afternoon after school, he walked past those same corners again. The Moe Town Rangers were out — dice flying, money flashing, cars bouncing low to the beat. It was like a movie on repeat, each day drawing him closer, each day teaching him the rhythm and rules of a life he hadn't yet chosen but couldn't resist.

Watching turned into conversations. Conversations turned into errands. Errands turned into a sense of belonging. They gave him a nickname, treated him like one of their own, and for the first time outside of his family, Theodis felt that rare, intoxicating sense of acceptance — a kind that came with risk and invisible contracts he couldn't yet understand.

The streets had rules, yes, but they also had rewards: fast respect, easy money, and the illusion of control. At that age, it felt like power. At that age, it felt like freedom.

Yet beneath it all, his grandmother's voice still echoed in his mind:

"Baby, don't let this world trick you. Time don't wait for nobody — not even the young."

He didn't understand it yet. But the streets would teach him soon. The choices he made now, the paths he followed, and the alliances he forged were shaping a lesson in permanence — one that would cost more than money or reputation.

Theodis was about to take his first real fall, and the weight of it would be heavier than he ever imagined.

CHAPTER EIGHT:

The Streets Claim a Piece

The days started to blur — same walk to school, same laughter with Dameon and Dante, same corner where the Moe Town Rangers ran the block like kings over a kingdom no one dared challenge. The older Theodis got, the more he saw the world for what it was — sharp, unforgiving, dangerous — and the more he realized that understanding it came with its own risks.

He would walk past the Rangers and watch carefully. Money changed hands in back pockets and sneakers. Dice bounced across cracked concrete like a heartbeat in rhythm with the city. Chrome rims spun slowly, deliberately, as if they had all the time in the world. It looked like success. It looked like respect. It looked like power. But Theodis was learning early that power always demanded a price — a price he hadn't fully calculated yet.

One Friday afternoon, school let out like any other, the air thick with the end-of-week energy — kids laughing, plans forming, sneakers drumming the sidewalk in rhythm. Theodis and Dameon decided to stop by the corner store before heading home. It was routine — a snack, some conversation, maybe a few jokes about the girls at school. Dante had detention that day and stayed behind, unaware of how that small, seemingly meaningless detail would shift everything.

The bell above the store door jingled when they walked in. Chips, candy, and soda filled the air with the comforting hum of normal life. But stepping outside, the normal dissolved instantly.

A car rolled up slowly, too slowly. Windows down. Music off. Silence stretched thick like smoke in the air. Theodis barely had a second to turn his head before the shots rang out.

Pop. Pop. Pop.

Then a pause.

Then more.

Instinct took over. He hit the ground, heart pounding, vision blurring. When he looked up, the world had stopped — and so had Dameon.

Still. Silent. Gone.

The city's pulse vanished. The laughter, the distant school bell, the rhythm of life itself — all drowned beneath the roar of his own heartbeat. He screamed his friend's name, shook him, begged him to move. But the street had already claimed its piece, right there in front of the store where they had stood countless times before, laughing, joking, dreaming.

That moment carved itself into Theodis' soul. Pain turned to anger. Anger hardened into purpose. He stopped simply walking past the Moe Town Rangers — he walked toward them. Life didn't need to recruit him; it had already. The grief, the rage, the helplessness — it all pushed him toward the one family that seemed capable of protecting him.

His mama, Bridget, had been seeing one of the Rangers — a man named Juniorbanks. Junior wasn't just another street figure; he carried presence, strategy, and earned respect with every move. He saw something in Theodis — the same fire, the same hunger that refused to be taught or restrained.

Juniorbanks took Theodis under his wing, teaching him the game the streets demanded — the money, the loyalty, the danger. Which moves paid off, and which got you buried? Every lesson came with a cost, every opportunity with risk. Juniorbanks became a teacher in a world that gave only consequences, not instructions.

Even as part of Theodis' heart still remembered Granny Flora's voice, the warmth of that crowded dinner table, he was already deep in the streets. The pull was too strong, the lessons too immediate, and the desire for survival too consuming.

The street had called him. And this time, Theodis answered.

He wasn't just a boy wandering anymore. He was a student of the game, learning that every choice carried weight, every alliance came with strings, and every step forward was a gamble.

Pain had found him, but it had also forged him. And now, there was no turning back.

CHAPTER NINE:

Blood in the Lesson

The first thing the streets teach you is how to survive.

The second thing they teach you is just how much that survival will cost.

After Dameon's death, Theodis' world hardened overnight. The laughter, the school days, the innocence — all vanished like smoke in the wind. Every step he took after that day carried a purpose: never feel powerless again. Never let loss define him the same way twice. Juniorbanks became more than a mentor — he became a guide through a world built on codes that came without rules, only warnings.

The Moe Town Rangers moved like a family, but a family forged in steel and shadows — built on silence, loyalty, and respect. They protected one another, but the world outside was dangerous and unforgiving. Every handshake carried meaning. Every nod weighed more than gold. Theodis learned fast: keep your eyes open, your words few, your emotions locked tight. Show weakness, and the streets will test you — sometimes violently.

Juniorbanks started with the small things: how to watch a corner, how to spot trouble before it erupted, how to move strategically while everyone else moved recklessly. But every lesson came with a shadow. The deeper he sank into the game, the more danger he attracted — not just from others, but from the very life he was learning to master.

Weeks became months. Theodis began earning respect. The same guys who once ignored him now treated him like he had always belonged. But with respect came a new kind of pressure. He was no longer the boy on the sidelines. He was a player, now expected to ride or fall with the crew.

Then came the night that changed everything.

The Rangers had a disagreement with another crew — a fight over territory, money, pride. Pride in the streets was volatile, and all it needed was one spark. Theodis was told to stay back, to watch and learn. But he couldn't. Some part of him refused to let his brothers go without him — not after everything he'd lost. So he went anyway. Quiet, alert, heart pounding but steady.

The argument started loud — voices shouting, threats thrown, a push here and there. And then — gunfire.

The shots tore through the night, sharp and fast. Theodis froze, eyes wide, chest hammering against his ribs. When the smoke cleared, a body hit the ground. Someone he knew. Someone from their own side.

The truth hit like a punch to the gut: the streets don't love anybody.

It didn't matter how loyal you were, how hard you fought, or how deep you rode — one wrong second, one misstep, and everything you believed in could vanish.

Juniorbanks pulled Theodis aside after that night. His face was cold, but his voice carried a weight heavier than the gunmetal sky.

"Lil D," he said, "you learning now. Out here, loyalty comes with blood. You don't get no medals for surviving — just memories that don't fade."

Theodis nodded, but inside, the lesson burned deeper than fire. That night replayed endlessly in his mind — the sound of the shots, the smell of gunpowder, the sickening weight of understanding that revenge never truly brings peace.

He had wanted power. He had wanted respect.

But what he got was something far heavier: real, lasting, unshakable pain.

Still, walking away wasn't an option — not yet.

Once the streets claimed a piece of you, they didn't release it easily. And sometimes, no matter how much you plan, life had its own rules. Sometimes things didn't go as planned — and you had to learn to survive anyway.

Pain became a teacher. Anger became fuel. Survival became instinct. And Theodis — hardened, hungry, determined — was ready to face the next lesson the streets had in store.

CHAPTER TEN:

Searching for Light in the Dark

Some nights, silence speaks louder than gunfire.

And for Theodis, those nights started coming more often — creeping up on him like shadows that refused to let go.

He'd sit alone on porches, street corners, even rooftops, letting the quiet wrap around him. No dice games. No late-night missions. No laughter from the Rangers. Just the kind of silence that forces a man to face himself... whether he wants to or not.

After the night one of his own fell, Theodis wasn't the same. Something deep inside his chest cracked — not loud, but enough to change the way he saw everything. He still rolled with the Moe Town Rangers, still carried their respect like a badge, but now every corner looked different. Every face had weight. Every sound felt like a warning.

He saw ghosts.

Dameon's smile.

The older guys he once looked up to.

People who'd been alive one moment and gone the next.

Juniorbanks saw the change too.

"You thinking too much, Lil D," he said one night, tapping ash off the end of his cigarette.

"Thinking'll get you hurt out here."

But Theodis didn't answer. Didn't argue. Didn't even blink.

He just stared up at the moon hanging above the block — bright, distant, untouched.

Maybe he wasn't scared.

Maybe he was something worse: tired.

Tired of funerals.

Tired of revenge.

Tired of pretending the streets were home when all they ever did was take.

He would go home some nights and sit in the old room he grew up in, the one his mama Bridget tried to keep untouched. Pictures of him as a kid were still there — photos in cheap frames, dusty but full of life.

Granny Flora's smile.

His grandfather's stern eyes.

His mama's arms holding him like she knew he'd one day face storms bigger than he could imagine.

The smell of home-cooked food, the noise of family, the safe warmth inside that little house — it all felt like another lifetime.

A memory wrapped in gold, fading because he'd walked too far from it.

In his sleep, he still saw Dameon.

Still heard him calling out, "We late for school, D! Come on!" Still jolted awake to the echo of gunshot memories.

Each morning, Theodis would face the mirror, trying to see the boy he used to be.

But that kid was gone.

Now he saw a man built from hurt, loyalty, survival — and the pieces of dreams he didn't know how to hold together.

The turning point hit him unexpectedly.

He was riding with Juniorbanks one night, cruising slow through familiar streets. When they stopped at a red light near Sherman Elementary, Theodis looked out the window and froze.

Kids were running around the playground — laughing, shooting hoops, chasing each other like the world didn't know violence, didn't know grief.

For a moment, he saw himself.

Him and Dameon and Dante walking down the sidewalk with backpacks, talking trash about who Poopye liked, dreaming about harmless things like sneakers and basketball and summer break.

Life before death touched his world.

It hit him like a brick to the chest — a silent reminder of everything that could've been.

"Junior..." Theodis asked quietly, eyes still on the kids, "you ever get tired?" Junior didn't look over. He just exhaled, the smoke trailing out the window.

"Every day, lil bro. But out here, tired ain't enough to stop you. Out here we keep movin'.

Always."

Theodis nodded, but something in his spirit cracked even more.

He didn't want to "keep moving" like this.

Not anymore.

Not if it meant losing himself piece by piece.

That night, instead of hitting the block, he went home. Sat on the porch alone. Let the cool air wrap around him like an old blanket.

He looked up at the stars — the same way Granny Flora used to when she prayed over her family.

He didn't know the right prayer.

He didn't know if God still listened.

But he whispered anyway:

"God... if you got somethin' else for me, show me. 'Cause I can't keep living like this." And for the first time in a long, long time...

He felt something.

Not peace.

Not forgiveness.

But a spark — small, fragile, fighting to survive inside all the darkness.

A spark that felt like hope.

He didn't know where it would lead him.

Didn't know what changes it would demand.

Didn't know if the streets would even let him go.

But he knew one thing:

He was done chasing shadows.

He was ready to start searching for light.

CHAPTER ELEVEN:

When Love Risks Everything

Change don't always start with a plan — sometimes it starts with love.

And in Theodis's world, love had always been rare, fragile, and unpredictable. But when it showed up, it had a way of turning everything upside down.

Life on the streets was pulling him deeper by the day, but back home, something unexpected was happening — something softer, something quieter, something that felt like the first break in a long cycle of pain.

Bridget & Juniorbanks — An Unlikely Kind of Healing

His mother, Bridget, had grown close to Juniorbanks, the same man guiding Theodis through the underworld. Their connection wasn't loud or dramatic — it grew slow, steady, and real, like two people who'd been tired of being alone for far too long.

Juniorbanks wasn't a saint. Streets raised him, carved him, and scarred him. He lived by instinct, caution, and silence. But around Bridget, that hardness started melting.

Where others saw a hustler, she saw a man who'd been forced to be strong for too long.

And she gave him something he hadn't felt in years — a place where he could breathe.

Bridget cooked for him after long nights, made sure he ate, and made sure he rested. Juniorbanks fixed things around the house, carried bags for her, and made repairs without being asked. They weren't just surviving together — they were healing together.

Everyone around them felt the shift, especially Theodis.

A New Home, A New Chance

When Bridget and Junior decided to move in together, it felt like life was trying to open a new door.

They found a home on 51st and Morgan — small, still in the hood, but full of possibility. The place wasn't perfect, but it had something Theodis hadn't felt in a long time: quiet. A new start. A place where hope could breathe.

At night, they'd sit at the table, talking in low voices about the life they wanted — a safer one, a lighter one.

Theodis would listen from his room, pretending to be asleep, but every word sat heavy in his chest.

One night, he heard Bridget's voice crack as she spoke.

"Junior... I don't wanna lose my son to these streets. I just can't. Not after everything we've been through."

Juniorbanks didn't jump to answer. He sat there for a long moment, rubbing his hands together — the gesture of a man who'd buried too many people to make promises lightly.

"I know, B," he finally said. "I don't want that either. Chicago been good to me... but it's taken too much too. Maybe it's time to think different."

That's when Bridget said the word that could change all their lives:

"Milwaukee."

She had cousins out there — a quieter city, slower pace, fewer bullets flying through the night. A place where Theodis could breathe without having to search every corner first.

Juniorbanks looked at her long and hard.

"If it means keeping him alive... I'll go. I'll leave all this behind." Theodis felt that line hit him deep.

He'd never heard a man like Juniorbanks talk about walking away — not for fear, not for greed, but out of love.

For his mother.

For him.

For the future they still had a chance to build.

The Weight of Walking Away

But leaving the streets ain't as simple as packing a bag.

The Moe Town Rangers didn't just let people disappear.

Once you're in, you're bound by loyalty — or trapped by it.

Theodis knew that if Juniorbanks tried to leave, someone would question it. Someone would challenge it. Someone might even try to test it.

And for the first time in his life, the idea of walking away scared him more than staying.

Would he lose the respect he fought for?

Would the streets retaliate?

Could he really leave behind everything he'd built — the reputation, the power, the protection?

But then he saw the way Bridget smiled when she imagined a new beginning — a smile he hadn't seen on her face since he was little.

He saw the way Juniorbanks stared out the window late at night like he was searching for a future he didn't think he deserved.

And slowly, a realization settled in Theodis's chest like truth.

Breaking the Cycle

All his life, he'd been taught to fight to survive.

Fight for his block.

Fight for respect.

Fight for revenge.

But for the first time, he saw a different kind of fight —

one that took more courage than picking up a gun.

He realized something powerful:

Sometimes the bravest thing you can do isn't fight to stay.

It's a fight to leave.

And Theodis knew deep down — this was his chance to break the cycle that swallowed so many before him.

A new city.

A new future.

A new version of himself. If he didn't take it now...

He might never get the chance again.

CHAPTER TWELVE:

Leaving the City

The morning they decided to leave Chicago, the city felt alive in a different way — like it knew something was shifting. The air was thick, heavy with the kind of silence that comes before a storm or a blessing. For Theodis, it felt like both.

This wasn't just a move.

This was an escape.

A gamble.

A chance at survival.

Bridget had made up her mind weeks ago. Juniorbanks too. But Theodis... he was torn between two worlds — the one that raised him and the one that wanted to save him.

The Plan Nobody Thought Would Happen

Milwaukee wasn't a dream. It was a lifeline.

Bridget's cousins already had a small house waiting — a quiet street, a clean porch, neighbors who waved. A place where gunshots weren't the soundtrack of the night, where a kid could breathe without checking over his shoulder.

But Chicago wasn't the kind of city you just "leave."

It had roots — deep ones — and Theodis had grown in the cracks between them.

Juniorbanks knew that better than anyone.

So he did the thing most men in his position feared:

He approached the Moe Town Rangers face-to-face.

A circle of hard faces watched him walk up — men who once respected him, feared him, followed him. Men Theodis had seen handle problems with bullets instead of words.

"Listen," Juniorbanks said, his voice steady as stone. "Ain't no beef. Ain't no betrayal. We leaving because the streets took enough from us. I'm protecting what's left." Some nodded.

Some frowned.

And one — a younger one with too much pride and not enough wisdom — said,

"Nobody leaves clean, OG. You know that."

Juniorbanks stepped forward, eyes locked, jaw tight.

"I'm not asking permission. I'm telling you the truth. A man got a right to save his family." Silence.

A long, dangerous silence.

In the end, no shots were fired. No threats were made.

But the message was clear — Some men were happy for him.

Others wanted to see him fall.

And that's the thing about leaving the streets:

You don't always know which one is waiting on your way out.

Packing Up a Past That Still Bleeds

The night before the move, the house on 51st and Morgan felt different — like every memory was standing in the rooms with them. Bridget moved slowly, folding clothes, wiping down tables, pausing every so often like she was saying goodbye to pieces of her life.

She touched the doorway where she marked Theodis's height.

She held the couch cushion with the faded stain from that night she dropped spaghetti, laughing too hard.

She ran her fingers along the window frame where she used to wait for her son to come home. It wasn't just a home — it was every hope she ever had for her boy.

"Theo," she said softly, her voice trembling, "I can't lose you to these streets. I can't bury another memory. Milwaukee... it's our lifeline, baby."

Theodis swallowed the lump in his throat and hugged her.

"I hear you, Ma. I do. I just gotta... let go of what I thought I'd be."

One Last Walk Through the Fire

That night, Theodis walked the block one final time. The city lights flickered against broken pavement. The corner store buzzed in the distance. Cars rolled by with slow, tinted windows, watching him like ghosts of every mistake he'd ever made.

He stopped at the exact spot Dameon fell.

The world was quiet here — too quiet.

He crouched down, touched the ground, and whispered,

"I ain't abandoning you, bro. I'm carrying you with me." The wind blew cold across his face.

Maybe it was nothing.

Maybe it was Dameon saying goodbye.

The Ride Out

At dawn, the car was packed.

Bridget is in the passenger seat, holding a photo of Granny Flora and Granddaddy Theodis Sr.

Juniorbanks focused on the road, jaw tight, eyes sharp — like he expected someone to try and stop them.

Theodis is in the back seat, watching the only world he ever knew fade into the rearview mirror.

No one talked for the first twenty minutes.

Not because they were scared — but because they knew the city wasn't done with them.

Not yet.

The skyline disappeared behind them, shrinking until it became nothing but memory.

Miles of highway stretched ahead.

More trees. More open space.

Less noise. Less danger.

For the first time, Theodis felt the weight lift — not all the way, but enough to breathe.

Halfway to Milwaukee, Bridget turned and smiled through tears.

"This right here... this is our second chance, baby."

Theodis nodded slowly, looking out the window at a world that didn't know his name.

For the first time in years, the future didn't feel like a threat.

It felt like hope.

But deep in his chest, he knew one truth the streets had carved into him: You can leave the city...

But the city doesn't always leave you.

CHAPTER THIRTEEN:

Shadows of Milwaukee

Milwaukee didn't look like a fresh start — it felt like one.

The air was lighter, the nights didn't hum with danger, and the silence wasn't something you had to fear. Still, Theodis moved through it like a man waiting to wake up from a dream. Peace was something he'd never learned to trust. Back home, quiet usually meant something was coming.

But Bridget kept her promise — a real chance, a real start.

She found them a small, warm apartment not far from Burbank High, tucked between rows of houses where kids rode bikes instead of running from sirens. Mothers sat on porches sipping coffee, old men swept their sidewalks, and families walked their dogs after sunset. It wasn't fancy, but it was safe — and safe felt brand-new.

The Building on the Corner

Every morning, Theodis walked the same route to school. And every morning, something tugged at his nerves.

On the corner before the long stretch toward Burbank High stood an abandoned building — a tall, rotting structure with boards nailed crooked over every window and paint peeling like dead skin. For reasons he couldn't explain, he always slowed down when he passed it.

It wasn't the type of building people avoided — it was the type they didn't look at. Like, even the locals were pretending it wasn't there.

And that made it worse.

New Faces, New Energy

A few days into the school year, Theodis met two brothers from the building next door — Leonard and Fudie. They were around his age, sharp, funny, and loud in a way that made quiet feel unnecessary. The kind of dudes you couldn't help but vibe with.

They walked with him every morning.

Joked about teachers.

Argued about who had the better jump shot.

Talked trash like they'd known him for years.

For the first time since he'd left Chicago, Theodis felt something familiar in his chest — belonging.

The Truth Behind the Boards

One morning, Leonard elbowed Theodis and pointed toward the abandoned building.

"You know what that is, right?"

Theodis shrugged. "Some raggedy spot somebody forgot about?"

Fudie snorted. "Nah, bro. That ain't just any building."

Leonard grinned, leaning in like he was telling a ghost story. "That's the apartment where Jeffrey Dahmer stayed. The building." Theodis froze mid-step.

He'd heard the name before — everybody had. A chill slipped down his spine, slow and cold.

"You serious?" he asked quietly.

"Dead serious," Leonard said. "They tore down most of it, but that piece right there... that's the one that stayed."

Fudie rubbed his arms like he had goosebumps. "Ain't nobody been in there for years, but people say you can hear things at night. Shuffling. Doors creaking. Like the walls remember." Theodis stared at the boarded windows.

Some places held pain.

He'd felt that before — on corners stained with blood, in houses that still echoed with arguments. But this... this was different.

This wasn't street danger.

This was evil — the kind that hides in plain sight.

And it shook him.

Because it reminded him that darkness didn't only live in people holding guns or running blocks.

Sometimes it lived in silence.

In loneliness.

In the mind of someone no one ever suspected.

Reflections in the Dark

That night, Theodis sat on his bed, looking out the window toward the faint outline of the building on the corner.

His thoughts drifted — to Dameon, to Chicago nights, to ghosts he carried from 51st and Morgan.

Then he thought about Dahmer — a man who looked normal, spoke soft, lived quietly... while hiding monsters in his soul.

That's when something clicked inside him.

Strength wasn't about how many people feared you.

Strength was surviving your own shadows — and choosing not to become one.

A Promise in the Dark

Staring at the dark shape of the abandoned building, Theodis made himself a promise:

He'd stay focused.

Stay aware.

Stay alive.

He had already seen what the world could do to good people — and what broken people could do to the world.

Milwaukee wasn't just a new beginning.

It was a test — one he was determined to pass.

Because he wasn't running from darkness anymore.

He was walking toward his own light — even if shadows followed close behind.

CHAPTER FOURTEEN:

Adjusting to a New World

Milwaukee wasn't Chicago, and Theodis felt that from the moment he stepped out of the car.

The city moved more slowly. The nights didn't vibrate with danger. People sat on porches, walked their dogs, and nodded hello even if they didn't know you. It was calm... almost too calm. After everything he'd lived through, peace felt strange on his skin.

Bridget was determined to make this move work.

She unpacked the house as her life depended on it — new curtains up the first night, food in the fridge, pictures on the walls before the boxes were even empty. Juniorbanks helped with the heavy lifting, joking to keep her from stressing too much.

But for Theodis, settling in wasn't that simple.

The Walk to School

On his first day walking to Burbank High, he kept his hood up and his eyes sharp. Old habits didn't die quick. He looked for corners, exits, who watched him, who didn't — the same survival skills he'd learned in Chicago.

Halfway down the block, he saw an old apartment building. Boarded windows, peeling paint, busted door. Not abandoned — just neglected. Milwaukee had spots like that, too. Areas where life was still rough around the edges.

Every morning he walked past it, he'd see men hanging outside — smokers, hustlers, guys who looked like they'd been dealt too many hard days. They didn't bother him, but they watched everything.

For Theodis, that building became a reminder:

You can change cities, but the struggle follows people just trying to make it.

New Faces, New Friendships

At school, he met Leonard and Fudie, brothers who lived in the building next door to his. Funny, loud, always arguing, but inseparable. They walked with him most mornings, showing him the easiest routes, the teachers to avoid, the girls who talked too much, and the ones who

didn't talk at all.

They kept things real, and they didn't treat him like an outsider. That alone made Milwaukee feel lighter.

"So you from Chicago?" Leonard asked one day.

"Yeah."

"That's why you walk like somebody always behind you," Fudie laughed.

Theodis smirked. "Chicago don't let you walk any other way." The brothers nodded. They understood more than they said.

The Neighborhood Reality

Milwaukee wasn't soft.

It had its own problems — different, but real.

You had kids skipping school to hustle on corners, families struggling to keep their lights on, and old heads arguing over dice games outside corner stores. Violence didn't happen every night like in Chicago, but when it did, it hit hard and unexpected.

One evening, while Juniorbanks was working late, Bridget heard a fight break out down the block. Two neighbors yelling, then glass breaking, then police sirens. She stood at the window, hands shaking slightly.

"Thought moving here would end this mess," she whispered.

Theodis came up behind her and placed a hand on her shoulder.

"Mama... it's better. Not perfect. But better."

She nodded, wiping her eyes.

Theodis vs. Himself

The hardest battle wasn't the city — it was what Theodis carried inside.

Sometimes he'd wake up at night thinking he heard Chicago sounds — gunshots, tires screeching, arguments outside his window. But when he opened his eyes, it was just Milwaukee's quiet.

He wasn't used to quiet.

At school, teachers noticed he stayed distant. He didn't raise his hand, didn't trust crowds, and didn't like it when people walked too close behind him. Trauma had a way of traveling with you, no matter where you went.

One day, his counselor asked him plainly, "What are you afraid will happen here?" He didn't answer right away.

Then he said, "Nothing here scares me... just what's still in my head."

The Building on the Corner

The old neglected apartment building continued to bother him — not because it was haunted, but because it reminded him of home in the worst ways. Men sitting outside drinking at 10 a.m., young boys watching them, learning the wrong lessons early.

One afternoon, as he walked by, a man yelled out:

"Aye, lil homie — where you from?"

Theodis stiffened. He recognized that tone.

"I ain't from nowhere," he answered calmly. "Just walking home." The man nodded slowly.

"Good. Keep it that way."

Theodis kept walking, heart steady but alert.

Milwaukee wasn't heaven — it had its own rules, its own dangers. But it wasn't Chicago either.

Here, he still had a chance to build something better if he stayed focused.

A Promise to Himself

That night, sitting in his room, he looked at an old picture — him and Dameon, smiling like the world couldn't touch them.

He whispered,

"I ain't wasting this chance. Not again."

For the first time since moving, he felt grounded.

Not running, not hiding — growing.

Milwaukee wasn't perfect.

But it was his reset button.

And he planned to use it right.

LSSTREETS.COM
S IN THE STREETS ITS HERE

CHAPTER FIFTEEN:

New Dreams, New Dangers — Rewritten

Sometimes the line between love and survival gets so thin, you can mistake one for the other.

Milwaukee had given Theodis and his family breathing room, but breathing room don't pay bills — and bills don't care what city you live in.

At first, life in Wisconsin felt different. Slower. Kinder.

Bridget had a steady job, Juniorbanks was working odd gigs, and Theodis was trying to stay focused in school. But peace can fool you — it can make you think you're safe, even when trouble is walking right back toward you.

It Started Small... Too Small to Notice

A call from Chicago here.

A "do me a favor" there.

A friend needing a ride... a package... a quiet handoff.

Nothing crazy. Nothing loud.

But small moves stack up like bricks — and before long, Juniorbanks and Bridget had rebuilt a whole operation without even announcing it.

This time, it wasn't corner work.

It wasn't wild, reckless moves.

It was organized. Quiet. Smart.

A tight pipeline from Chicago to Milwaukee — cocaine, cash, and connections.

People who trusted Juniorbanks. People who respected Bridget.

People who never asked too many questions because they already knew the answers.

Bridget wasn't the type to sit back and hope things worked out.

She kept books tight, communication clean, and the whole operation under control. She didn't just help — she became the backbone.

Theodis noticed the shift.

He noticed the nights getting later.

The conversations getting shorter.

The money coming in faster.

He wasn't a kid anymore — he knew what he was seeing.

But for the first time in a while, he saw something else too: his family moving as one.

Not broken. Not fighting. Just... building.

New Temptations, New Voices

One night, Bridget sat at the table talking on the phone with her sister Christine from Minnesota.

Christine didn't sugarcoat anything.

She said:

"Milwaukee small-time. If you really want to make money, you gotta come up here. Ain't nobody touching the market. It's wide open." Bridget listened quietly.

She didn't agree, didn't disagree — but her eyes said enough.

She was thinking.

Dreaming.

Planning.

Juniorbanks didn't know it yet, but the seed had already been planted.

A Change of Heart

Before Bridget could bring up Minnesota, Juniorbanks made a move that shocked everyone.

One night, after dinner, he called her into the living room.

His voice wasn't confident like usual — it was shaky. Real.

He got down on one knee.

"Bridget... you been my peace when all I knew was war. I wanna build something permanent with you. Will you marry me?"

Bridget didn't answer at first — she cried.

Then she nodded, laughing and crying at the same time, hugging him like she never wanted to let go.

Theodis, watching, felt something strange:

Hope.

Real hope.

A Wedding Nobody Expected

When the wedding day came, it felt like two worlds collided.

Families from St. Louis, Arkansas, Detroit, Atlanta, Chicago, and Minnesota all packed the halls.

Music everywhere.

Tables full.

Kids running, aunties dancing, uncles talking loudly like always.

Even the Moe Town Rangers — the heads, the top dogs — pulled up wearing suits that barely fit their personalities. They weren't there for business.

They came out of respect for Juniorbanks, for Bridget, and for the life they were trying to build.

For one night, the world really did stop spinning.

For one night, nobody was running.

Nobody was watching their back.

Nobody was burying anything — not pain, not fear, not pride.

Theodis stood in the corner, watching everyone smile, laugh, and celebrate.

He felt something warm in his chest.

He didn't know the world could still hold moments like this.

Then Reality Hit Back

After the wedding, life went right back to normal — meaning dangerous, unpredictable, and constantly shifting.

Bridget kept talking more about Minnesota.

Christine kept putting the opportunity in her ear.

More money.

Less heat.

More room to build something big.

Juniorbanks fought the idea at first.

He liked Milwaukee.

He understood Milwaukee.

But deep down, he knew staying still too long could get a man killed.

So after a few heated nights, a few risky last runs, and a few prayers whispered when nobody was listening...

They made the decision.

Milwaukee Was No Longer Home — Just a Memory

Boxes packed.

Furniture sold.

Goodbyes said.

Another city left behind.

Another chance ahead.

As they drove out of Milwaukee, Theodis stared out the back window just like he had leaving Chicago.

One city disappearing behind him.

Another city waiting ahead — Minneapolis, Minnesota.

He didn't say a word, but a feeling sat heavy in his chest:

Every move was bigger.

Every risk was greater.

Every dream was louder.

But danger?

Danger was always right there too — never too far, never too silent.

He didn't know it yet, but Minnesota wouldn't just change its address.

It would change the entire direction of his life.

Forever.

CHAPTER SIXTEEN:

Family, Flash, and New Roads

Rewritten

The move to Minneapolis was supposed to be a fresh start — and for a while, it felt like exactly that.

The city buzzed with energy, alive in a way Milwaukee never had been. Streets filled with opportunity, people walking fast, ambition in their eyes. Bridget and Juniorbanks arrived ready to take it all on, carrying their small victories and larger dreams. But this time, they weren't completely alone — family was already waiting.

Uncle Sporty, Bridget's younger brother, was the first to welcome them.

Sporty wasn't just surviving — he was thriving.

Every time you saw him, he looked untouchable. Suits tailored to perfection, gold chains glinting with every gesture, diamond rings catching light like little stars on his fingers. His walk was confident, his words precise, and his style screamed success. But beneath all the flash was a man who knew the streets just as well as he knew a balance sheet.

Sporty ran a towing company, owned corner stores, and managed a network of side hustles that kept him one step ahead of both the law and rivals. Yet when Bridget and Juniorbanks arrived, Sporty didn't flaunt it — he welcomed them like family first, boss second.

"You home now?" he said with a grin, wide and real. "Ain't no reason we can't all eat together. Table's set."

And they did exactly that.

The meals were heavy with flavor, laughter bouncing off the walls. Money moved through the household in quiet, precise ways — checks, deals, investments — but none of it felt dangerous, at least not yet. For Bridget, it was a relief. Finally, she felt the weight of her life lift a little.

Security didn't come often, and when it did, it was worth savoring.

Restlessness Returns

But even in the middle of all that comfort, the old tension gnawed at her.

The streets don't just disappear because you change cities. Business never runs perfectly smooth. Whispers came — small, offhand, but sharp: police attention, rival players watching too close, unknown dangers shadowing their success.

Bridget had built too much to risk it all again. She'd lost too much. Every move carried consequences, and she wasn't about to ignore them.

Then the call came from her sister, Christine, up in Rochester.

"Bridget," Christine said, voice calm but insistent, "come stay here for a while. It's quiet. Safe.

Bring Theodis. Let the kids grow up around family, not chaos."

The words hit differently this time. Minneapolis had its appeal, sure, but Christine offered something else: roots. Stability. A place where Theodis could just be a kid, without looking over his shoulder at the shadows that always lurked nearby.

Bridget thought long and hard. She loved Sporty, respected his grind, but her heart knew it wasn't the right long-term home. After ten months of Minneapolis — of late nights, endless business meetings, luxury cars lined up like trophies — she made the call. They packed up again.

Rochester: A Different Kind of Life

Theodis didn't know it yet, but this move would change him.

When they arrived in Rochester, Christine's house exploded with life. Kids screaming, laughter ricocheting off the walls, cousins running like wind to greet him. Dibbles, Swift, Script, and Kyna — old friends, playmates, allies — all enveloped him as if no time had passed.

These cousins weren't just family — they were comrades of childhood wars and victories. The kind of bond forged through scraped knees, secret adventures, backyard battles, and whispered confessions late at night.

Now older, they picked up right where they left off. Endless talks, laughter until midnight, and a kind of family loyalty that made every risk, every move, every sacrifice worth it.

Rochester wasn't flashy. There were no gold chains or luxury cars to impress neighbors. There were no high-stakes deals waiting around every corner. But for Theodis, it didn't matter. The value wasn't in what you could see — it was in the love surrounding him, the foundation beneath his feet, the security that didn't depend on the streets.

And though Theodis didn't know it yet, this choice — this decision to return to family, to find safety and grounding — would shape the next chapter of his life in ways nobody could have predicted.

Because sometimes, the biggest moves aren't the flashy ones.

Sometimes, the moves that change everything are the quiet ones, the ones that build a life worth living.

For Theodis, Rochester was more than a city.

It was the first real chance to be free.

CHAPTER SEVENTEEN:

Learning the Game

Rochester was quieter than Chicago, calmer than Milwaukee, but Theodis quickly realized — the streets never really left you. They adapt. They evolve. And if you wanted to survive, you had to adapt right along with them.

The city had its own rhythm, its own hierarchy, and its own players — smaller corners, tighter crews, but the same rules applied: respect was earned, trust was scarce, and mistakes came with consequences. Theodis had learned some of this in Chicago and Milwaukee, but Rochester felt different — smaller, sharper, more intimate. Here, everyone knew everyone else, and every move could echo.

His older cousin, Kyna, became his guide in this new world. She was only a year older, but she carried herself like someone who had already fought her battles. Rough, confident, and fearless, Kyna had already earned respect with the older crew in town. She showed Theodis and Swift how to move carefully, how to read people, and how to make money without drawing the wrong attention. Every lesson came with subtle warnings: "Watch your back, know who's watching you, and never let them see fear."

Dibbles was right behind them — a storm in motion. Aggressive, impulsive, testing boundaries, eager to prove himself. He had fire, but sometimes it burned the wrong way. And then there was Script, the youngest, quieter, and more cautious. He observed everything, taking mental notes while staying out of trouble. He wasn't always in the action, but his sharp eyes caught things others missed — patterns, weaknesses, opportunities.

Theodis followed Kyna like a shadow. Every errand, every corner, every handshake became a lesson in strategy. She taught them the small moves first: how to handle small deliveries, how to read the streets, how to earn respect without stepping on the wrong toes. But beneath all that was a larger goal — legacy. Kyna made it clear: "Money comes and goes. Respect and brains?

That stays. You move smart, you survive. You move dumb, you don't."

Kyna's crew was tight, and each member taught a lesson in their own way:

- Ricky — sharp, quick, always thinking two steps ahead, a strategist who could predict the flow of any situation.
- TG — bold and loyal, never scared to confront threats head-on.
- Don Don — muscle and presence, the kind of person everyone listened to without question.
- Latifa — brains behind the operations, organizing moves, keeping records, and thinking five steps into the future.
- Lord, Stoney, and Landa — the eyes and ears of the streets, each specializing in intelligence, messaging, and situational awareness.

Theodis and Swift watched them like live tutorials — how they walked, how they talked, how they moved. Every gesture, every word, every choice mattered. It was more than survival; it was learning the chessboard of the streets.

Meanwhile, the adults in the family — Bridget, Juniorbanks, and the rest of the heads — ran the larger operations with quiet precision. Their business was legal enough on the surface to avoid attention, but the feds were never far. Surveillance, notes, informants — the tension was always there, a reminder that one misstep could bring everything crashing down.

For Theodis, this was his first real taste of responsibility. The weight of his family's legacy pressed on him. Every corner he walked, every message he ran, every interaction carried consequences. One slip, one poorly timed move, and it could unravel years of work, trust, and protection his family had built.

But it wasn't just fear driving him. There was excitement, too. The thrill of learning, of proving himself, of carving a place in a world that demanded skill and strategy. Each lesson — from reading body language to counting cash, from spotting law enforcement to measuring loyalty — sharpened him.

By the end of his first month in Rochester, Theodis wasn't just a kid from Chicago anymore. He was a student of the streets, learning the rules, testing his limits, and understanding the stakes. He could feel himself changing — moving more deliberately, thinking ahead, protecting those around him, and, for the first time, considering what it meant to lead.

The streets of Rochester were different from any he'd known before, smaller but deadly in their precision. And in that environment, Theodis learned one of the hardest truths: survival wasn't just about strength or speed — it was about brains, timing, and respect.

By the time the sun set on that first month, Theodis understood something profound: he wasn't just surviving anymore. He was learning. And soon, he would have the power to shape the game itself.

CHAPTER EIGHTEEN:

Testing Boundaries

By the time Theodis had settled into Rochester, he was no longer the wide-eyed kid from Chicago. He had learned the streets' rhythm, studied the players, and started understanding how power flowed — but learning didn't mean he was untouchable.

Kyna had made it clear: respect was earned, trust was fragile, and mistakes were costly. But Theodis felt the pull of youth, the desire to test his limits. He wanted to see if everything he'd learned could hold up in real life — if he could step into the bigger game without failing.

One Friday evening, Kyna's crew had a small operation running in a quiet corner. Theodis and Swift were tasked with running messages, picking up cash, and observing — nothing flashy, nothing risky. But for Theodis, it was a chance to measure himself.

The corner was alive with low voices, the shuffle of shoes on cracked pavement, and the occasional car rolling past. Theodis counted, watched, and memorized every face. He knew which neighbor watched too closely, which cars belonged to friendly crews, and which could spell trouble.

Then he noticed him — a kid from another block, maybe two years older, trying to move in on Kyna's corner. He wasn't violent, not yet. Just testing, showing off, claiming a little territory.

Theodis felt the adrenaline surge. He could step back and let Kyna's crew handle it. That would have been the smart move. But he felt the pull to assert himself, to show that he was more than just a student.

"Yo," he called out, his voice calm but firm. "This corner's not yours. Step back."

The kid laughed, sizing him up. "You gonna stop me, lil boy?"

That's when Theodis realized — respect wasn't about fear. It wasn't about how loud you were or how flashy your crew. It was about composure, timing, and the willingness to risk what mattered most to protect it.

Before things escalated, Kyna appeared, walking toward them with Swift, Ricky, and TG in tow. One look from her, and the tension shifted. The other kid smiled nervously and stepped back, recognizing the unspoken code — this crew wasn't to be messed with.

Theodis felt the rush of triumph, but Kyna clapped him on the shoulder. "Good instincts," she said. "But remember — testing boundaries can get you killed. You learned today, not just how to talk, but when to walk away. That's the real game."

Later that night, Theodis sat on the porch of Aunt Christine's house, thinking about what had happened. He wasn't scared — he was alive, alert, and sharper than before. But he knew the truth: the streets didn't forgive mistakes, and pride was a dangerous teacher.

That moment marked a shift. Theodis realized that leadership wasn't about proving you could fight or run; it was about controlling yourself, observing, and knowing when to act — and when not to.

He made a quiet promise to himself: he would keep learning, keep testing his limits, but never lose sight of what mattered most — family, survival, and respect earned the right way.

The game was bigger than him, but for the first time, he felt like he could play it on his terms.

CHAPTER NINETEEN:

Rising Tensions

Rochester had felt like a second chance, but even the quietest streets carry shadows. For Theodia and Swift, life had started to feel like a high-stakes game — one where losing wasn't an option. Under Kyna's watchful eye, they learned fast. Small hustles turned into bigger moves, corners became territories, and respect had to be earned every single day.

But with power came attention — and not all of it good.

The feds weren't sleeping. For months, they had eyes on the family, tracking shipments, following accounts, noting every unusual movement. Bridget and Juniorbanks ran things quietly, but no matter how careful they were, the law had a habit of creeping in silently, waiting for one wrong move to hit.

And the rival crews were relentless. Hungry, desperate, and fast, they wanted the influence Kyna's crew had carved out. Ricky, TG, Don Don, Latifa, and the others had handled small skirmishes before, but now the stakes were higher — blood, pride, and territory were all on the line.

Theodia and Swift were no longer observers. They were active players — running errands, scouting corners, reporting movements, watching every step. One slip, one wrong glance, and the consequences could come from rivals or the law.

One late afternoon, on what was supposed to be a routine drop, Theodia noticed a car parked too long near Kyna's favorite corner. Its driver moved with precision, scanning the block as though he owned it.

"Yo, Theo," Swift whispered, leaning in, "that dude been here too long. Somethin' ain't right."

Theodia's stomach tightened. The same rush he'd felt on the streets of Chicago — the one that had kept him alive through ambushes and chaos — washed over him. He and Swift held back, watching every movement. Then, two men stepped out, eyes sharp, walking toward the corner with a confidence that set off alarms in his chest.

The rivalry had just escalated.

Kyna's crew arrived shortly after, alert, scanning the block. Voices clashed, tempers flared, and for a few tense minutes, the air felt like it could snap. Swift's aggression came out immediately, but Theodia caught him just in time. Every second mattered — one fight here could draw the feds in or spark something far deadlier.

By nightfall, no one had been hurt, but the message was clear: the rivals were watching, the law was watching, and every corner, every move, every deal had to be calculated. Mistakes weren't just costly — they could be fatal.

That night, Theodia and Swift climbed to the rooftop of their apartment, the city spread below like a map of opportunity and danger.

"Man," Swift said, shaking his head, "it's like they everywhere. Ain't no peace anywhere."

Theodia stayed quiet, thinking. He thought about Kyna, the crew, his cousins, his family — everyone counting on him to stay sharp, to survive.

"You right," he finally said, voice steady. "But we learn. We adapt. We move smarter. We don't let the streets break us. Not now. Not ever."

Swift nodded slowly, understanding. The stakes had risen, but so had their awareness. They weren't just surviving — they were learning how to dominate without getting caught in the chaos.

The night air was cold, but the city pulsed beneath them, alive with possibilities. Theodia knew the next moves would define them — one misstep, and everything could crumble. But for the first time, he felt ready. Not just to survive, but to rise — smarter, sharper, and stronger than ever.

CHAPTER TWENTY:

Chaos at Kyna's

Rochester was supposed to be a fresh start, but nothing in Theodia's life had ever stayed calm for long.

With Aunt Christine and her husband Duke locked up, their four kids had moved in with Bridget. The house was packed, chaotic, and heavy with responsibility. Every day felt like a balancing act — school, chores, money, and keeping the younger cousins safe.

Kyna, once a guide and anchor, was gone. She wanted freedom — her own apartment, her own rules. For Theodia and Swift, it became an invitation to the edge.

No curfews. No rules. No one to hold them back.

At first, it felt like freedom. Kyna's apartment became their world: the kitchen smelled sharp with chemicals, the counter held scales, and the thrill of handling product gave them a sense of power they'd never had. They were learning fast — how to weigh, package, and move — absorbing the streets' harsh lessons from someone who had lived them every day.

Bridget tried to enforce boundaries, but Theodia and Swift ignored her. The younger cousins stayed home, structured and safe. They chose chaos. They ran toward independence.

Eventually, they left Bridget's house entirely, moving into Kyna's apartment permanently.

Kyna was rarely there. She had her crew to run, her moves to make. That left Theodia and Swift in charge — hosting friends, girls, anyone they trusted. It felt intoxicating. Dangerous. Thrilling.

But every high came with risk.

And then, one night, the cost came due.

Shots erupted. The sound shredded the calm of the night. Screams bounced off the walls. Chaos swallowed the apartment whole. Theodia's body reacted before his mind could — he shoved Swift behind a counter, ducked low, and ran. Bullets tore through the walls near him. Glass shattered. Blood spattered. Fear and adrenaline fused into a storm that drove him forward.

He didn't stop until he reached Charlie's house, an old friend from Rochester with a calm presence that could steady anyone in trouble. Charlie didn't ask questions. He stripped Theodia of his blood-soaked clothes, cleaned him up, and pressed a new set into his hands.

"Go back to Chicago," Charlie said, voice quiet but firm. "Lay low. Stay alive. Don't look back."

Theodia didn't argue. He left in the middle of the night, riding the bus as the city lights blurred past him. Every mile was heavy with thought, fear, and adrenaline. For the first time in months, he realized just how close he'd come to losing everything.

Chicago hit him like a weight he hadn't felt in years — familiar, dangerous, alive. He was heading to his biological father, James, a man he hadn't seen in years. For now, it would be a refuge — a place to hide, to heal, to think.

Blood on his clothes. Chaos in his mind. The streets calling.

Theodia understood one thing clearly: life had changed forever. Every choice from here on carried consequences. One slip could cost him everything.

And the streets? They were patient. Waiting. Watching. Ready to remind him of that truth — brutally and without mercy.

CHAPTER TWENTY-ONE:

Back in Chicago — High Stakes

Chicago didn't welcome him. It tested him. The city he'd once called home now felt like a stranger — streets familiar but strange, corners whispering danger instead of nostalgia. Every echo seemed to remember him, every shadow reminded him he'd survived before... but barely.

Stepping off the bus, Theodia's chest tightened. The weight of his choices, the mistakes, the streets he'd walked — all pressed down. He was back under his father James's roof, but the house wasn't a sanctuary. It was quiet, too quiet, like the calm before a storm.

James was the same man he'd always known — distant, restless, chasing something invisible.

The house barely held life, except for Troy, James's patient, steady wife, and Shabrina, Theodia's older sister. Troy moved like a shield, providing safety and structure without judgment. Shabrina became his secret anchor. They talked late into the night, trading memories, regrets, and dreams of escape. It was the first time Theodia felt seen in weeks.

But peace in Chicago was always a mirage.

Whispers had traveled fast. From Rochester, from the streets, from the feds — all tracing back to the shooting at Kyna's apartment. Theodia hadn't fired a gun, hadn't pulled a trigger, yet his name was painted across every report. Loyalty had a price, and guilt clung to him like blood.

And then came the betrayal that left a scar deeper than any street fight.

Late one night, the silence of the house was broken not by footsteps, but by absence. His jewelry — pieces of memory, pieces of pride — gone. James had taken them. When confronted, his father denied it, face tight, unflinching, pretending nothing had happened.

The truth, as always, found a way to crawl out.

Sherry, James's niece, cornered him quietly. "I seen him," she whispered, eyes flicking around as if the walls had ears. "I saw James take your jewelry."

It wasn't about the gold, the chains, or the rings. It was about trust, respect, safety — the things a home was supposed to guarantee. And in that moment, Theodia's last sliver of respect for his father disintegrated.

He grabbed his phone with hands that trembled but didn't shake enough to hide the resolve.

"Ma," he said, voice sharp, low, trembling, "I don't wanna be here no more. I can't. I wanna come home."

Bridget didn't hesitate. She came through the night, pulled him from the chaos, eyes steady, words measured — the kind of calm that carried the weight of knowing you'd always fight for your child.

The drive back to Rochester was silent, filled only with the hum of tires on the asphalt. The city shrank behind them, but the streets, the family, the chaos — all waited ahead. Only this time,

Theodia felt different. He was sharper, harder, and more alert.

And then, he met Aaliyah. She didn't just step into his life — she entered like a challenge, a lesson, a light he didn't know he'd been chasing.

A new chapter had begun. Not just survival. Not just streets. But connection. Strategy. Love. And the knowledge that every choice from here on carried the weight of consequences... and danger.

Chicago hadn't let him go, but maybe this time, he'd learn to move first.

CHAPTER TWENTY-TWO:

First Child, First Betrayal – The Legacy Begins

Dating Aaliyah had been everything Theodia didn't see coming — a mixture of fire, intrigue, and a challenge he didn't know he wanted. For two months, they were inseparable, grinding together, navigating life, hustling side by side, and discovering each other's truths in a world where trust was rare and fleeting.

But Aaliyah carried secrets, layers hidden behind her confident smile and city-smart charm. She told him the woman she lived with was her mother — a lie. He soon found out she was on house arrest for theft, a past carefully stitched into the present. She blended street knowledge with a small-town survival instinct, a combination that intrigued and unsettled him.

Despite the deception, Theodia was drawn in. There was something magnetic about her — a spark he couldn't ignore. A fire he wanted to protect, a life he wanted to share. For the first time, he considered a world outside the streets, outside the grind — a life that wasn't just survival.

Their connection deepened. Intimacy became their language, their bond stronger than words.

And then came the news that shifted everything: Aaliyah was pregnant.

Theodia's heart skipped, then fell heavy with the weight of responsibility. This wasn't just about him anymore. This child carried a piece of him, a piece of his blood, a piece of his legacy. He felt a surge of protectiveness, the kind of responsibility no street lesson or money ever prepared him for. He wanted to provide, to nurture, to shield this new life from the chaos he had known too well.

Together, they began planning. Grinding. Saving. Dreaming. For a while, they stayed with Bridget and Juniorbanks, who welcomed them without judgment, offering a roof over their heads while they built toward a future that didn't include fear at every turn.

But life, as it always did, tested them.

One day, Theodia told Aaliyah he had to make a short trip to Chicago, promising he'd return in a few days. But when he came home earlier than planned, the world he had been carefully building cracked wide open.

The sight that met him would etch itself into his memory forever: Aaliyah in Don Don's arms.

Betrayal struck sharper than any bullet, heavier than any street fight. In that instant, Theodia understood something about loyalty, love, and survival: sometimes, the streets taught lessons even the heart couldn't avoid. He felt rage, heartbreak, and disbelief all at once. He would never trust her again.

Yet the child changed the rules. This tiny life, growing inside Aaliyah, demanded a different kind of strength — one Theodia couldn't ignore. Walking away was no longer an option. He couldn't abandon this legacy, this piece of himself.

So they decided — carefully, painfully — to move forward. Not with blind trust, not with illusions, but with purpose. Together, they worked to build a safe space, a sanctuary for their child. Until their apartment was ready, they leaned on Bridget and Juniorbanks, drawing strength from family, learning patience, and preparing for the life about to enter the world.

Theodia reflected on everything he had been through — Chicago, the streets, the grief, the chaos, the betrayals, the lessons. And now, he realized something vital: survival wasn't just about freedom anymore. It wasn't only about money, respect, or avoiding the dangers that had shaped him. Survival was about legacy — the people who depended on him, the family he would protect, the child he would raise.

Every day became a lesson in responsibility. Every choice mattered more than ever. He was building something beyond the hustle, beyond the streets — a life rooted in love, resilience, and hard-earned wisdom.

And as Aaliyah rested, unaware of the storm that raged inside him, Theodia made another silent promise. He would protect his child, provide for his family, and rise above the betrayals and chaos that had defined his life for so long.

For the first time, he saw the road clearly: the grind would never stop, the streets would always whisper, but now he had something stronger guiding him — purpose.

The streets had given him lessons, the streets had given him pain, but now, Theodia realized, the streets had also given him clarity. Survival was no longer enough. Legacy was the goal.

And with that, the real grind began — for love, for family, and for the life he would build with the one thing that mattered most: his child.

The streets might never forget him. Life might never be simple. But Theodia Martell Henry was ready.

This was the final chapter, the beginning of everything that truly mattered.

EPILOGUE:

Shadows Never Sleep

Years passed, but the streets never forgot Theodia. No matter how far he moved, no matter how much he tried to build a new life, the past had a way of creeping back — in the phone calls, in the whispers, in the cold stares of people who remembered his name.

He had a child now — a piece of him that demanded he fight harder, think smarter, survive longer. But the lessons he learned in Chicago, Rochester, Milwaukee, and Minneapolis had taught him one unshakable truth: freedom is temporary, and loyalty can turn to a knife in your back faster than you can blink.

He kept moving. He kept grinding. But every corner held danger, every deal carried risk, and every handshake came with a shadow he couldn't escape. The city streets were alive — not with music and laughter anymore, but with silent threats, coded warnings, and people who would kill to hold their power.

Some nights, Theodia walked alone, staring at the skyline, thinking about Dameon, the friends he'd lost, the betrayals he'd survived. The city whispered back, a constant reminder: there is no peace for people like him. Only moments of quiet between storms.

Aaliyah betrayal was still a scar, a lesson etched deep into his chest. He didn't hate her anymore — the streets had taught him that hate is wasted energy. He didn't trust easily, not anymore. Every relationship, every bond, every move was measured. Every choice had weight.

Every mistake had consequences.

The child grew up fast, surrounded by love and protection, but even innocence couldn't hide from reality. Theodia watched as the streets tried to pull the next generation in, the same way they had pulled him. And he understood something chilling: the cycle doesn't end. It never does. You survive, you rise, but the world keeps testing you.

One night, standing on a rooftop overlooking the city lights, Theodia lit a cigarette. Smoke curled in the cold air, drifting into the night like the ghosts of his past. He thought about everything he'd lost, everything he'd gained, and everything he'd risked.

The streets didn't care about his wins. They didn't care about his family. They only cared about survival, power, and respect — and he knew he'd have to keep paying the price every single day, in every way he could.

And as he watched the city pulse below him, alive and dangerous, Theodia smiled grimly. He was still here. Still breathing. Still fighting. Still learning that sometimes surviving wasn't enough — sometimes you had to walk through hell and come out sharper, harder, and unbroken.

The streets had claimed pieces of him, tried to break him, and whispered promises of death and betrayal. But Theodia? He had learned the only truth that mattered: life was real, raw, and unforgiving — and so was he.

The shadows never slept, but neither did he.